We hope you enjoy this book.
Please return or renew it by the due date.
You can renew it at **www.norfolk.gov.uk/libraries**
or by using our free library app. Otherwise you can
phone **0344 800 8020** - please have your library
card and pin ready.
You can sign up for email reminders too.

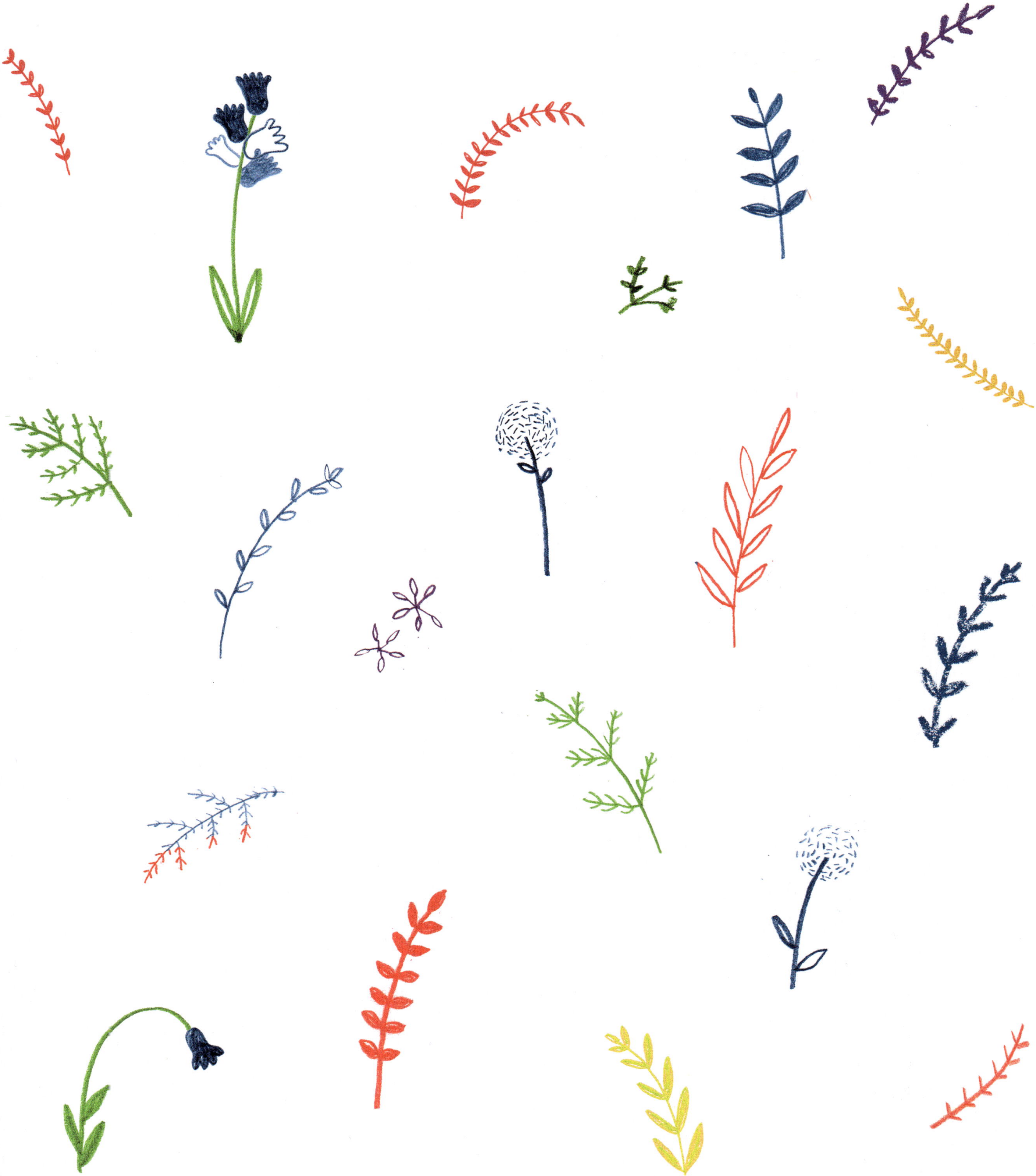

For Mum, Dad and Pea
—A.D.

First published in 2019 by Scholastic Children's Books
Euston House, 24 Eversholt Street, London NW1 1DB
a division of Scholastic Ltd
www.scholastic.co.uk
London ~ New York ~ Toronto ~ Sydney ~ Auckland
Mexico City ~ New Delhi ~ Hong Kong

Text and illustrations copyright © 2018 Anna Doherty

ISBN 978 1407 18173 8

1
2
3
4
5
6
7
8
9
10

The moral rights of Anna Doherty have been asserted.
Papers used by Scholastic Children's Books are
made from wood grown in sustainable forests.

STICKY

ANNA DohErty

SCHOLASTIC

The trouble began when
Badger was wrapping
Owl's birthday present.
This **particular** roll
of sticky tape was …

...particularly
sticky!

He tried peeling ...

and PULLING ...

But it was  use.

Badger was ...

Nothing

was

going

right.

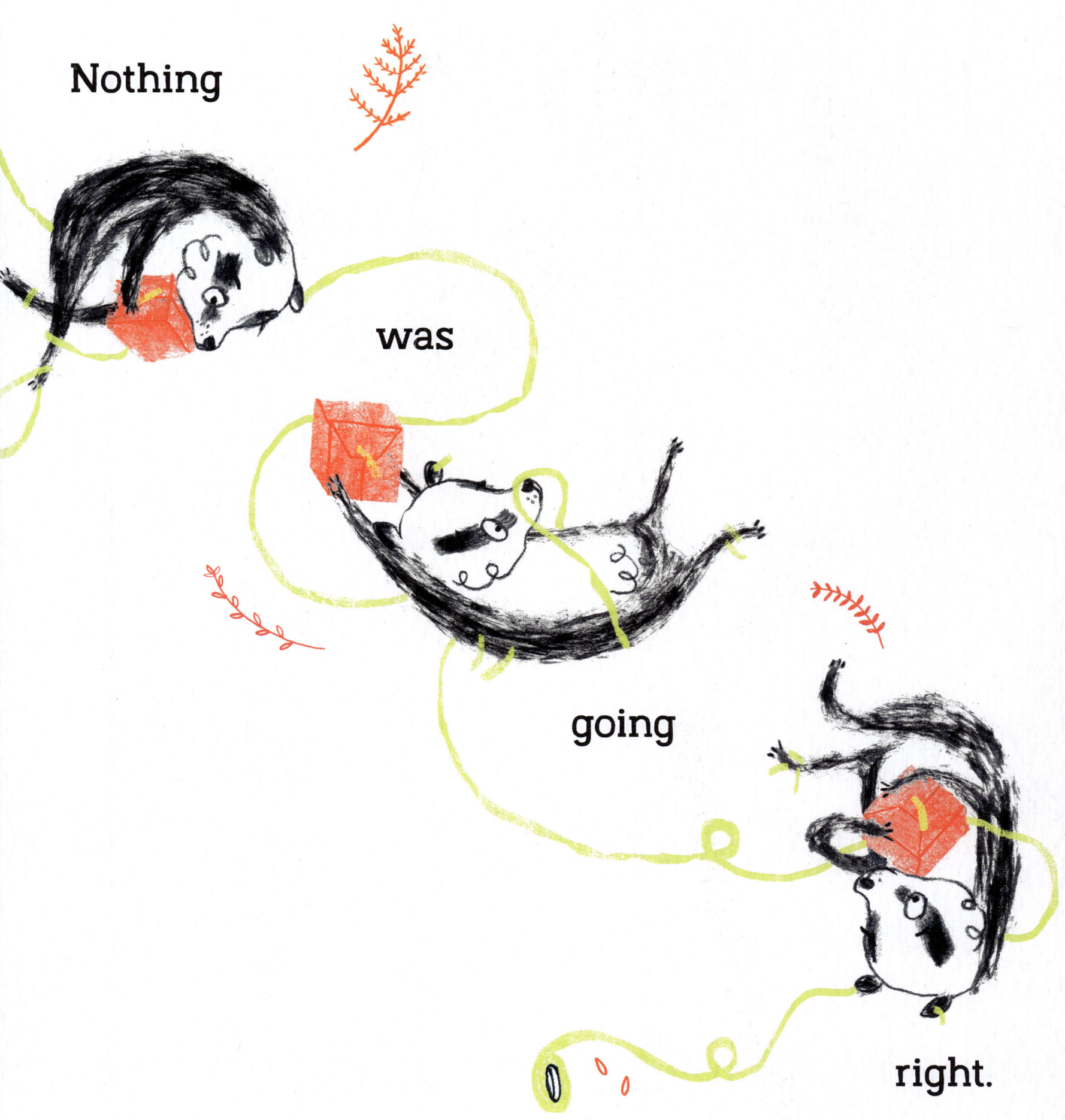

"Can I lend a helping hoof?" asked Deer.

"YES, PLEASE!"

said Badger.

However, hooves were NOT as helpful

Luckily, Rabbit was
keen to assist.

as Deer had hoped.

"Don't worry,
Rabbits are
very good at
getting out of
sticky situations."

But it seemed that rabbits   were NOT

very good

at getting

out of

sticky situations, after all.

"Need a paw?"
asked Mouse.

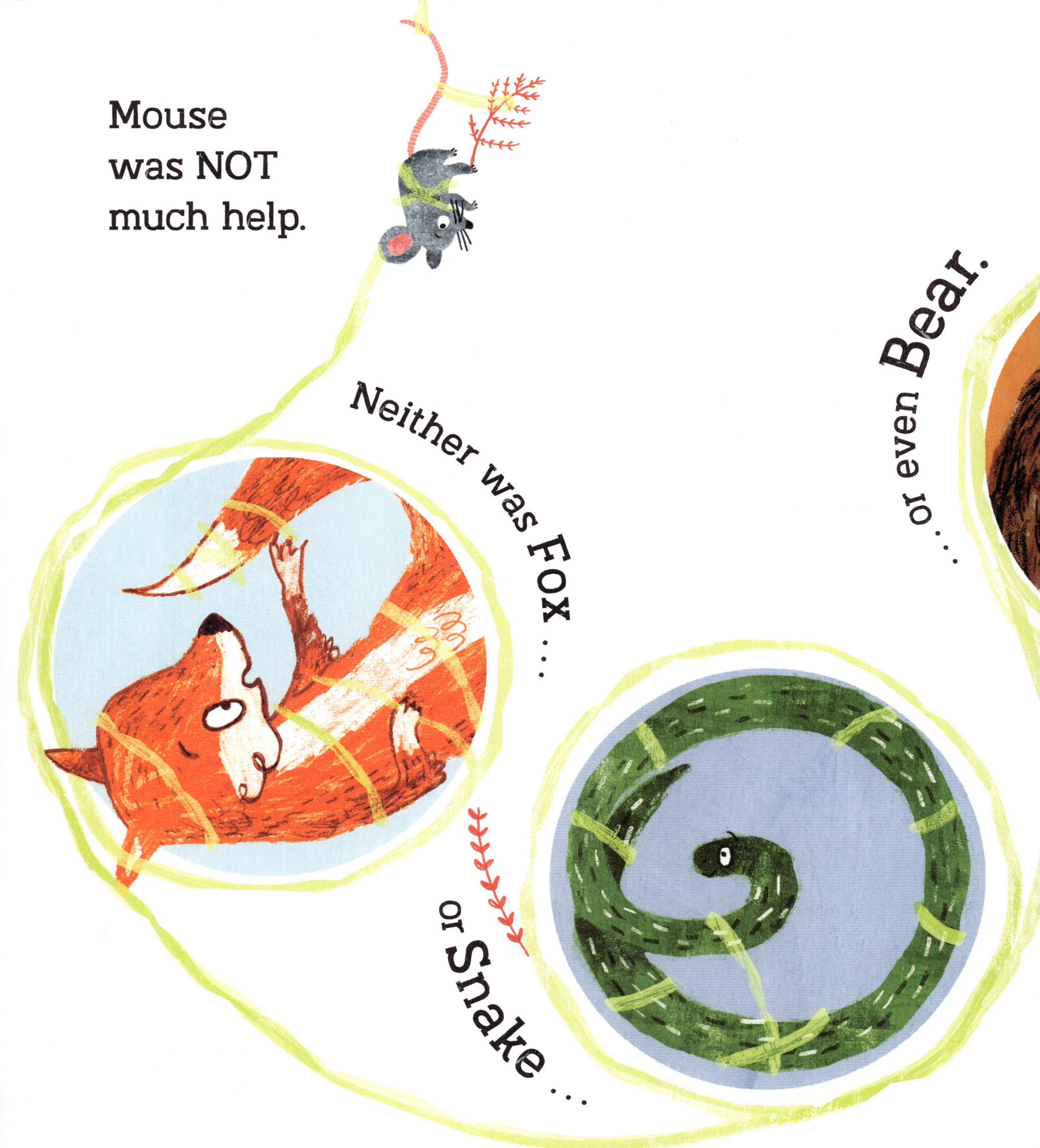

Mouse
was NOT
much help.

or even **Bear.**

Neither was Fox …

or **Snake** …

In fact, soon

EVERYONE

was **stuck!**

Finally, along came . . .

... OWL!

"Happy Birthday! We have your present here, but it's a little bit ... **stuck**,"

said Badger.

So with one last enormous effort

the animals peeled, tugged,

pulled and nibbled,

until the present ...

...came **free!**

"**SCISSORS!**" said Owl.
"What a perfect present!
I love them!"

"And THANK YOU...

. . . for **sticking around** to help me use them!"

Badger went home.
It was Mouse's birthday next week,
and he thought he might start . . .

. . . wrapping her present.

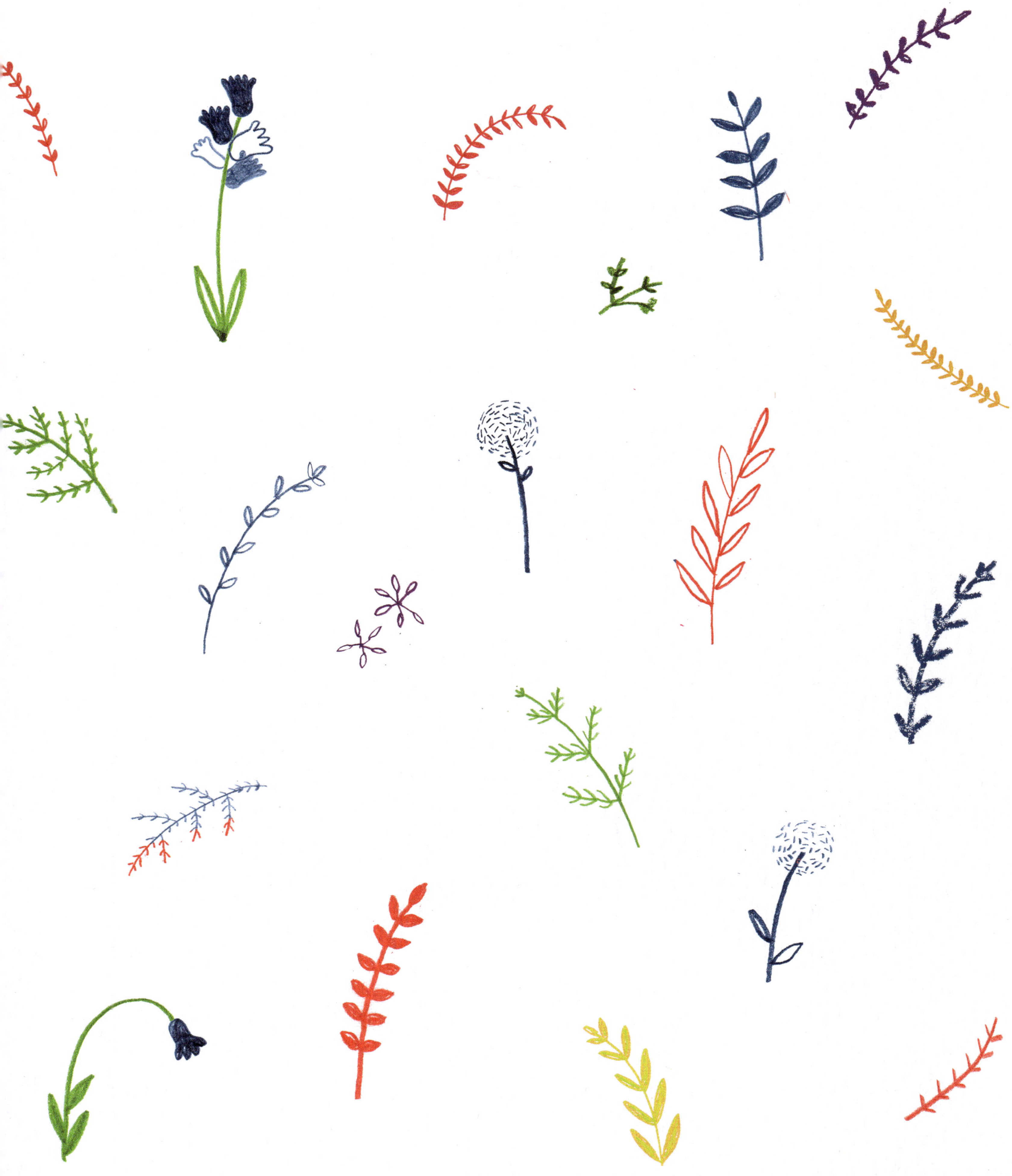